an

MON

additi

John K

THIS IS IT!
THE PICTURE THAT'S GOING TO GET ME MY FIRST FRONT PAGE. A REAL-LIFE VAMPIRE EXPOSED!

THE EDITOR IS GOING TO LOVE IT!

TOP TEN CONSPIRACY THEORIES

WHO KILLED COCK ROBIN?
Conspiracy and Cover-up

I BELIEVE!

SPOON BENDING FOR BEGINNERS

MOLENSKI

THE DAILY ROAR

NAME:
MONTY J. MOLENSKI
EMPLOYEE NO: 054567
D.O.B.: 9TH FEBRUARY
YEAR OF THE MOLE

ACE ~~JUNIOR~~ REPORTER

A Templar Book
First published in the UK in 2006
by Templar Publishing.
This softback edition published in 2007
by Templar Publishing, an imprint of
The Templar Company plc,
Pippbrook Mill, London Road,
Dorking, Surrey, RH4 1JE, UK
www.templarco.co.uk

First softback edition

ISBN 978-1-84011-127-9
Printed in Hong Kong

HONESTLY! MY TALENTS ARE ENTIRELY WASTED AT THIS RAG OF A NEWSPAPER. THE EDITOR IS REJECTING MY 'VAMPIRE EXPOSED' STORY. SAYS SHE WAS JUST A HARMLESS OLD LADY. AS IF! HE REALLY CAN BE A LITTLE BULL-HEADED AT TIMES. THOUGH MUST ADMIT, THE PICTURES I SNAPPED DIDN'T COME OUT QUITE AS PLANNED. MUST GET MY CAMERA FIXED — THINK IT'S ON THE BLINK.
THE DAILY ROAR
ILL-FATED FE
CAKE COMPETITION E
IN CONTAMINATIO
Ace reporter Chris Croc brings you a slice of the act
CAKE FÊTE
DANGER: KEEP OU

"BRING ME A PROPER STORY!" SNORTED THE EDITOR. "CHRIS CROC GOT HIS THIRD FRONT PAGE IN A WEEK! STOP WASTING YOUR TIME LOOKING FOR ALIENS AND SPOOKS THAT DON'T EXIST. GET OUT THERE AND FIND A REAL STORY — THEY'RE GOING ON RIGHT UNDER YOUR NOSE!"
HUH. SPOOKS DON'T EXIST, INDEED. WHAT PLANET'S HE FROM? I'VE YET TO PROVE THAT THEY DO, THAT'S ALL.

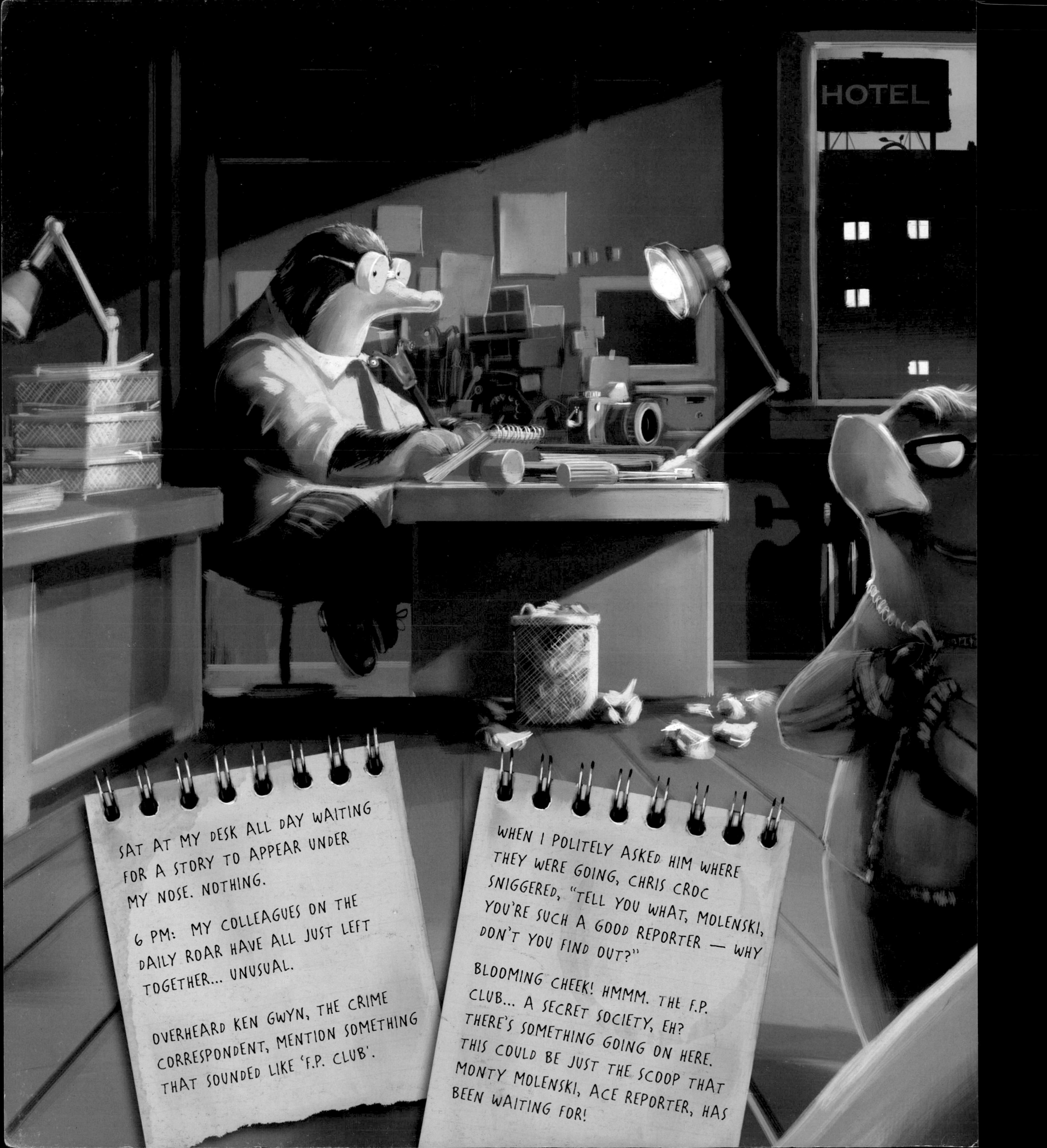
HOTEL
SAT AT MY DESK ALL DAY WAITING FOR A STORY TO APPEAR UNDER MY NOSE. NOTHING.
6 PM: MY COLLEAGUES ON THE DAILY ROAR HAVE ALL JUST LEFT TOGETHER... UNUSUAL.
OVERHEARD KEN GWYN, THE CRIME CORRESPONDENT, MENTION SOMETHING THAT SOUNDED LIKE 'F.P. CLUB'.
WHEN I POLITELY ASKED HIM WHERE THEY WERE GOING, CHRIS CROC SNIGGERED, "TELL YOU WHAT, MOLENSKI, YOU'RE SUCH A GOOD REPORTER — WHY DON'T YOU FIND OUT?"
BLOOMING CHEEK! HMMM. THE F.P. CLUB... A SECRET SOCIETY, EH? THERE'S SOMETHING GOING ON HERE. THIS COULD BE JUST THE SCOOP THAT MONTY MOLENSKI, ACE REPORTER, HAS BEEN WAITING FOR!

I CUNNINGLY OBSERVED THEM FROM THE OFFICE WINDOW AND WAS SURPRISED TO SEE THEM SIMPLY CROSS THE ROAD TO THE GRAND HOTEL! THE SHEER NERVE OF IT! HOLDING THEIR SECRET 'F.P. CLUB' MEETING RIGHT ON THE PAPER'S DOORSTEP. THEY PROBABLY THINK THAT'S THE LAST PLACE ANYONE WOULD LOOK.
I'VE GOT TO GET INSIDE THAT BUILDING AND FIND OUT WHAT THEY'RE UP TO.
HACKS AGAINST T
NOTORIOUS "FOUL POSSE CL
CAUGHT RED-HANDE
Bad guys banged to writes by ace reporter, Monty Molensk

THE DAILY ROAR

SCOOP!

NO BULL! ROAR DEAL FOR EDITOR EXPOSED AS MEMBER OF THE "FAKE PERSON CLUB"

Top reporter, Monty Molenski, takes the bull by the horns!

THIS IS IT!
MY BIG CHANCE FOR A SCOOP!

SECONDS LATER I WAS OUTSIDE THE HOTEL.
SECURITY WAS TIGHT: A CLEAR SIGN THEY MUST BE UP TO NO GOOD.
THE DOORMAN DIDN'T BUDGE AN INCH WHEN I SHOWED HIM MY PRESS PASS, THE BIG KNUCKLEHEAD!

MAURICE
French Chef
JUST MADE A COUPLE MORE INGENIOUS ATTEMPTS TO GET IN, BUT TO NO AVAIL.
EVEN MY 'EDUARDO SUAVO'S A CAPPELLA DISCO' DISGUISE DIDN'T WORK. I'M GOING TO HAVE TO RESORT TO OTHER MEANS OF ENTRY.
A-HA! I'VE SPOTTED AN OPEN WINDOW. HURRAH!

PARKING FOR HOTEL GUESTS ONLY
PIGS MIGHT FLY
Coming soon to
THE GREEN DOOR
click!
Big SHOES for BIG FEET!

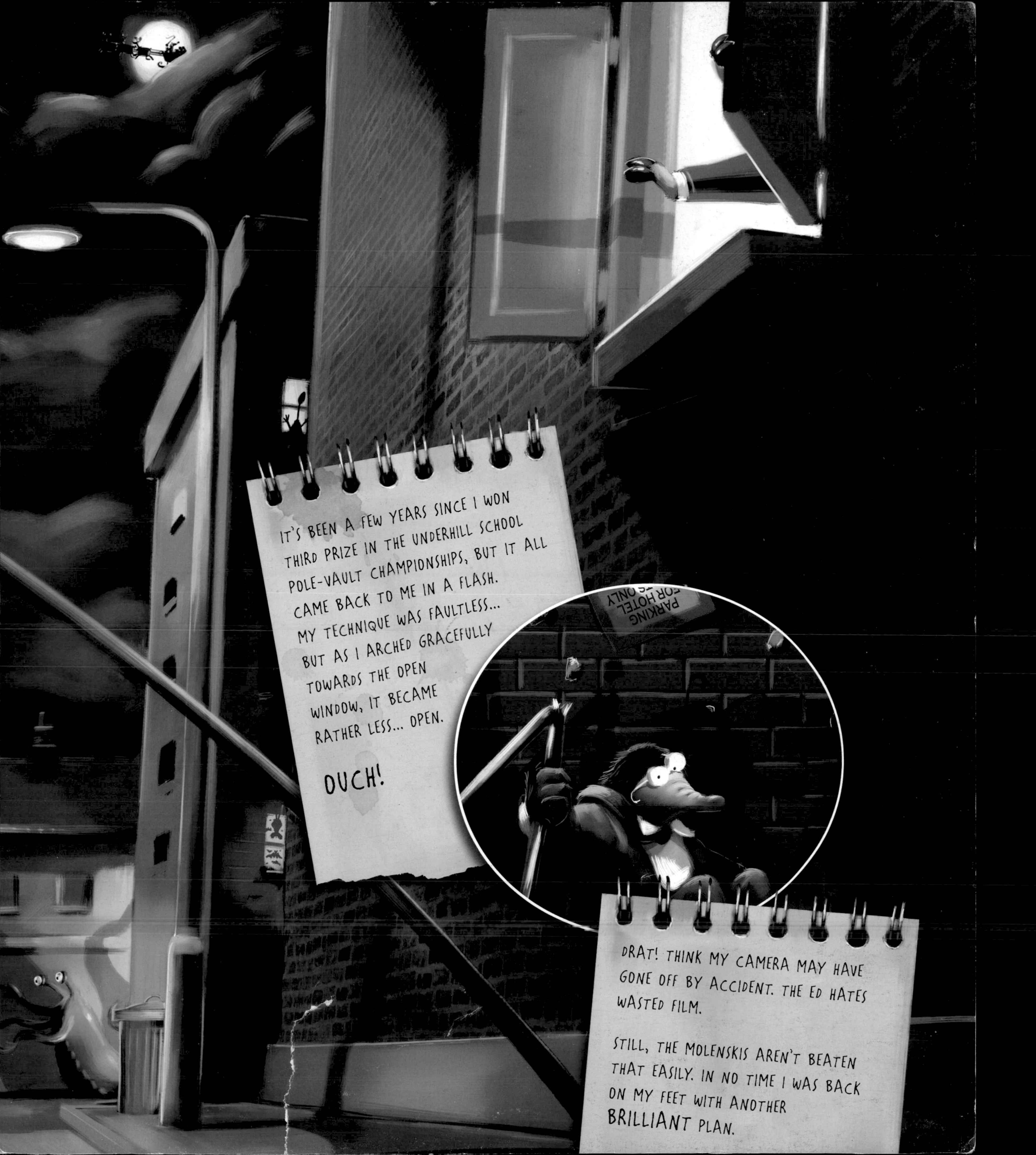
IT'S BEEN A FEW YEARS SINCE I WON THIRD PRIZE IN THE UNDERHILL SCHOOL POLE-VAULT CHAMPIONSHIPS, BUT IT ALL CAME BACK TO ME IN A FLASH. MY TECHNIQUE WAS FAULTLESS... BUT AS I ARCHED GRACEFULLY TOWARDS THE OPEN WINDOW, IT BECAME RATHER LESS... OPEN.
OUCH!
DRAT! THINK MY CAMERA MAY HAVE GONE OFF BY ACCIDENT. THE ED HATES WASTED FILM.
STILL, THE MOLENSKIS AREN'T BEATEN THAT EASILY. IN NO TIME I WAS BACK ON MY FEET WITH ANOTHER BRILLIANT PLAN.

click!
THE DAILY ROAR
IT'S A GRAVE MATTER!
WE'RE SICK TO DEATH!
STOP THE SEANCES
GIVE OUR BONES BACK!

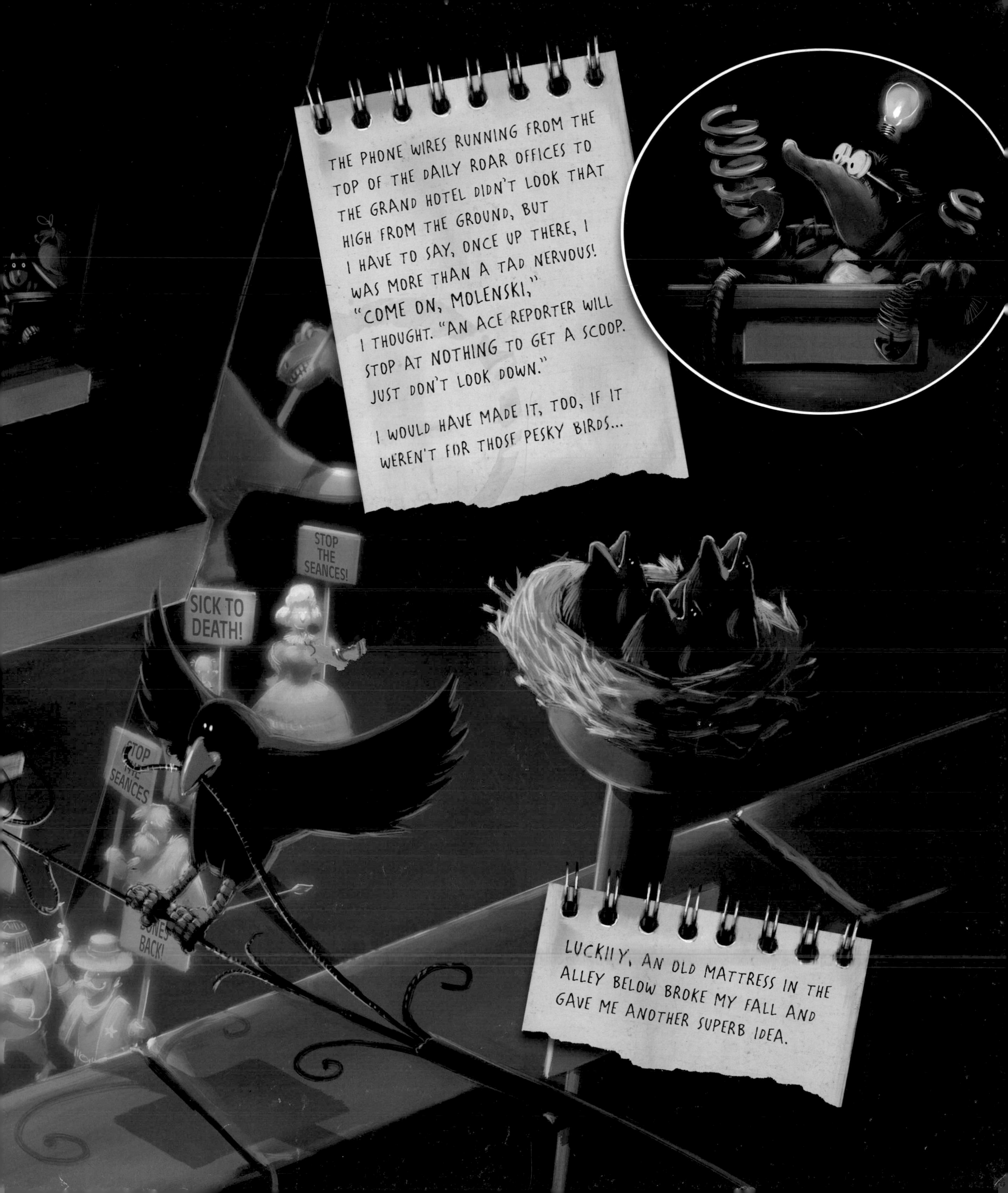
THE PHONE WIRES RUNNING FROM THE TOP OF THE DAILY ROAR OFFICES TO THE GRAND HOTEL DIDN'T LOOK THAT HIGH FROM THE GROUND, BUT I HAVE TO SAY, ONCE UP THERE, I WAS MORE THAN A TAD NERVOUS!
"COME ON, MOLENSKI," I THOUGHT. "AN ACE REPORTER WILL STOP AT NOTHING TO GET A SCOOP. JUST DON'T LOOK DOWN."
I WOULD HAVE MADE IT, TOO, IF IT WEREN'T FOR THOSE PESKY BIRDS...
STOP THE SEANCES!
SICK TO DEATH!
STOP THE SEANCES
BONES BACK!
LUCKILY, AN OLD MATTRESS IN THE ALLEY BELOW BROKE MY FALL AND GAVE ME ANOTHER SUPERB IDEA.

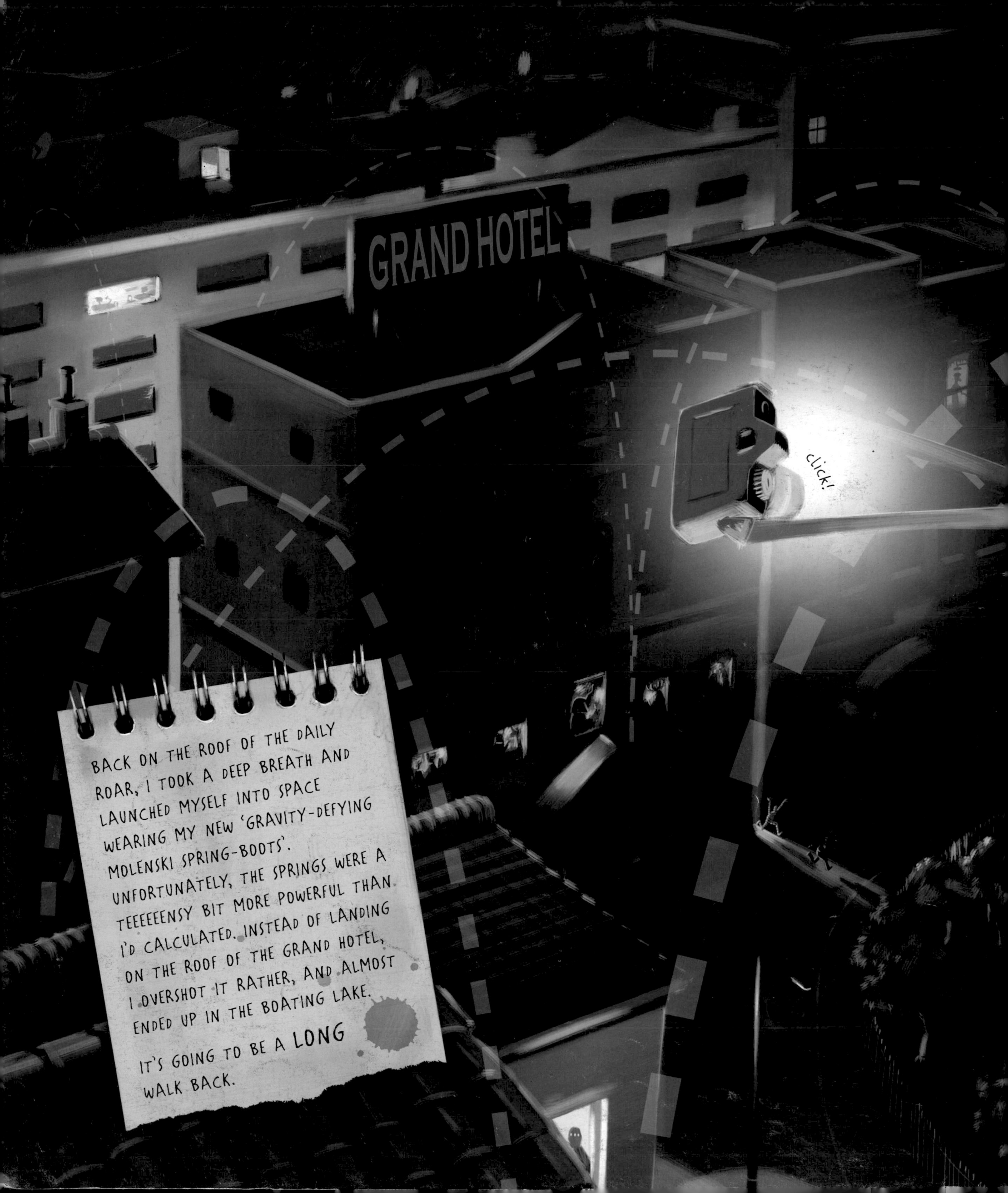

GRAND HOTEL

click!

BACK ON THE ROOF OF THE DAILY ROAR, I TOOK A DEEP BREATH AND LAUNCHED MYSELF INTO SPACE WEARING MY NEW 'GRAVITY-DEFYING MOLENSKI SPRING-BOOTS'. UNFORTUNATELY, THE SPRINGS WERE A TEEEEEENSY BIT MORE POWERFUL THAN I'D CALCULATED. INSTEAD OF LANDING ON THE ROOF OF THE GRAND HOTEL, I OVERSHOT IT RATHER, AND ALMOST ENDED UP IN THE BOATING LAKE.

IT'S GOING TO BE A **LONG** WALK BACK.

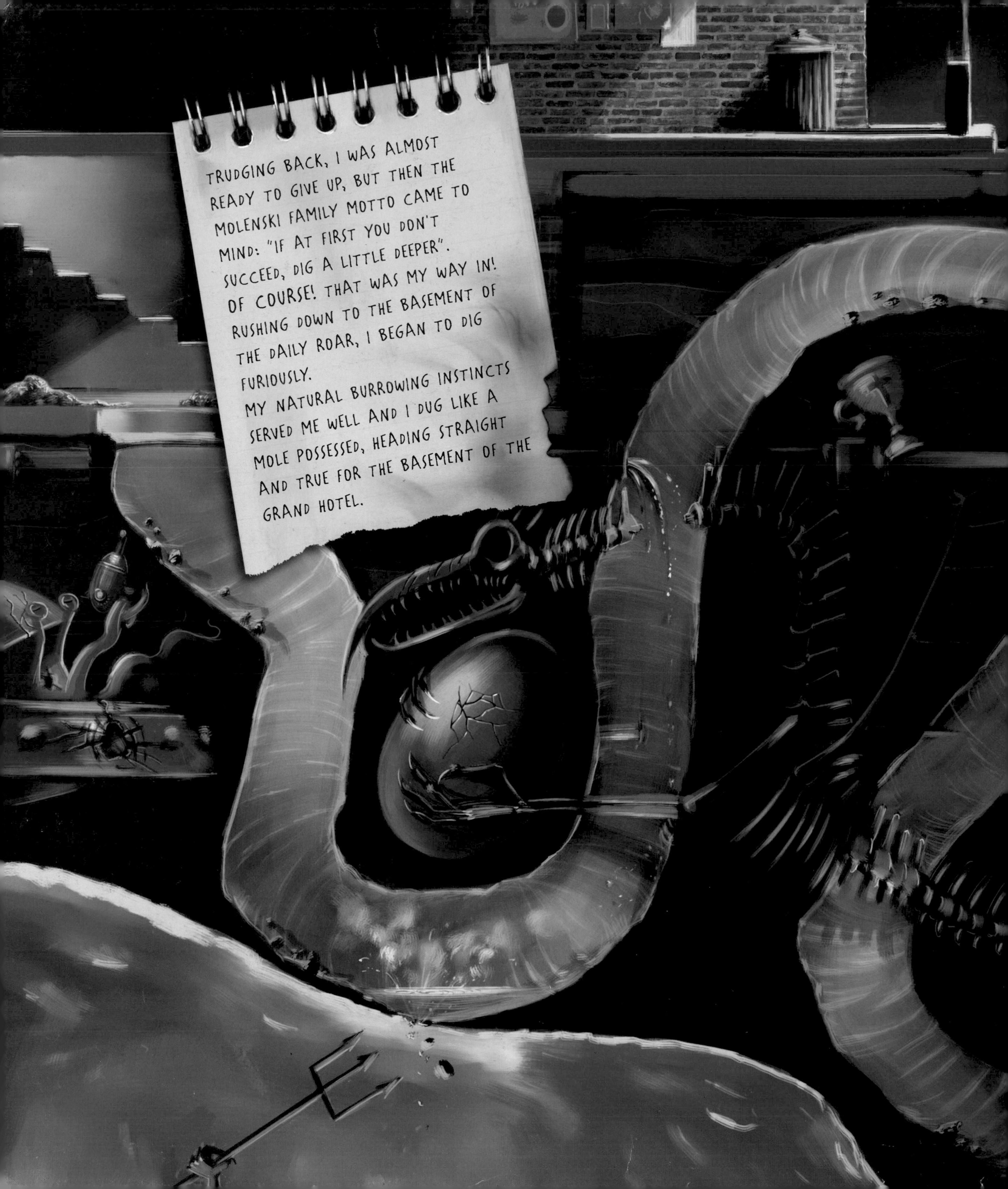
TRUDGING BACK, I WAS ALMOST READY TO GIVE UP, BUT THEN THE MOLENSKI FAMILY MOTTO CAME TO MIND: "IF AT FIRST YOU DON'T SUCCEED, DIG A LITTLE DEEPER". OF COURSE! THAT WAS MY WAY IN! RUSHING DOWN TO THE BASEMENT OF THE DAILY ROAR, I BEGAN TO DIG FURIOUSLY.
MY NATURAL BURROWING INSTINCTS SERVED ME WELL AND I DUG LIKE A MOLE POSSESSED, HEADING STRAIGHT AND TRUE FOR THE BASEMENT OF THE GRAND HOTEL.

HMPH. MUST HAVE MADE A TINY MISCALCULATION. I EMERGED BREATHLESSLY JUST SHORT OF THE HOTEL FRONT DOOR —
BACK WHERE I STARTED!
...BUT FOR ONE, WONDERFUL DIFFERENCE. THE HOTEL DOOR WAS OPEN! AT LAST, HERE WAS A CHANCE FOR A GLIMPSE OF THE SECRET MEETING!

I ZOOMED IN ON THE HOTEL'S OPEN DOORWAY...
BUT JUST AS I TOOK THE SHOT, SOME FOOL WITH BIG HAIR IN AN ENORMOUS FLASHY CAR PASSED STRAIGHT IN FRONT OF MY LENS.
ARGH! ANOTHER WASTED SHOT!

click!
EP

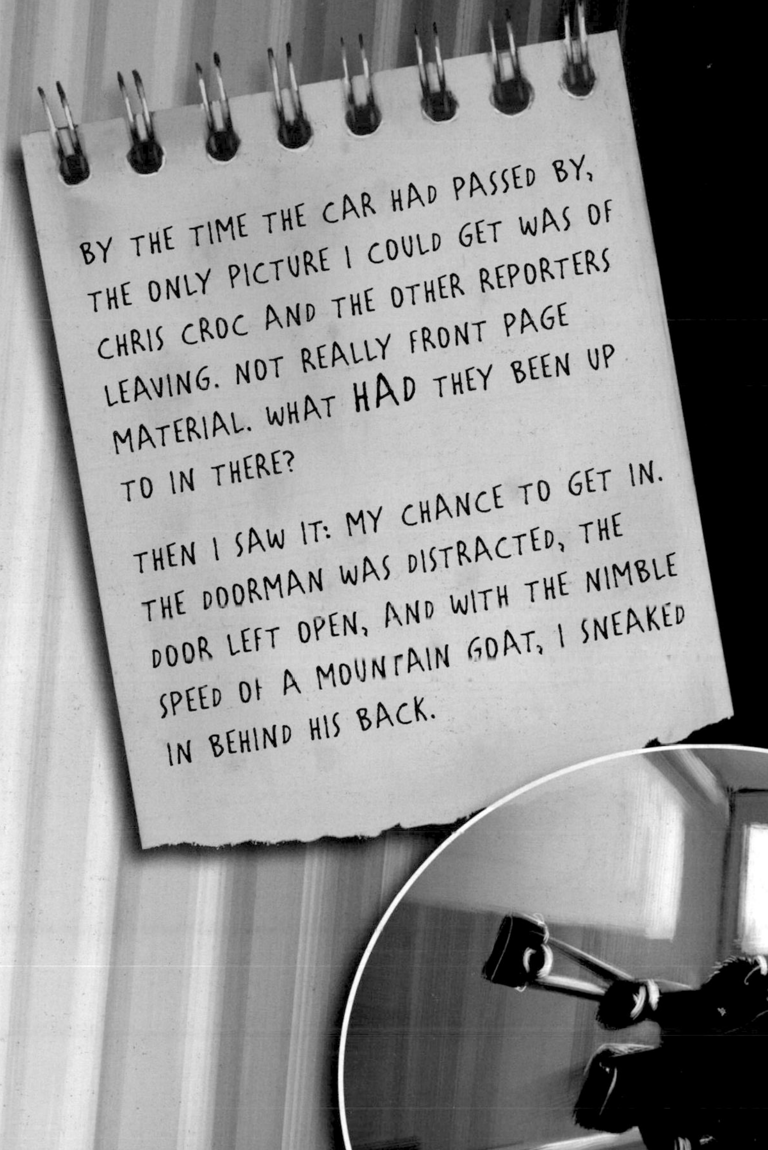

BY THE TIME THE CAR HAD PASSED BY, THE ONLY PICTURE I COULD GET WAS OF CHRIS CROC AND THE OTHER REPORTERS LEAVING. NOT REALLY FRONT PAGE MATERIAL. WHAT **HAD** THEY BEEN UP TO IN THERE?

THEN I SAW IT: MY CHANCE TO GET IN. THE DOORMAN WAS DISTRACTED, THE DOOR LEFT OPEN, AND WITH THE NIMBLE SPEED OF A MOUNTAIN GOAT, I SNEAKED IN BEHIND HIS BACK.

THE MYSTERY IS ABOUT TO BE SOLVED!

THE DAILY ROAR
SCOOP!
TO BEE OR NOT TO BEE...
BRITISH QUEEN UPSET AT HONEY SHORTAGE!
Top reporter, Chris Croc, gets the buzz!

AH. THE FRONT PAGE CLUB.
SO THAT'S WHAT 'F.P.' STANDS FOR.
OH, DEAR.

DARKROOM

THE DAILY
ROAR

ALL CAMERAS
MUST BE LEFT
HERE FOR
OVERNIGHT
PROCESSING
-THE NITE OWL

THOROUGHLY FED UP.
RETURNED TO THE DESERTED
DAILY ROAR OFFICES TO DROP OFF
MY CAMERA AT THE NITE OWL'S
FILM DEVELOPMENT LAB AS USUAL.

WHAT A WASTE OF TIME.
OH, WELL. HOME TO BED.

THE DAILY
ROAR
PHOTO DEVELOPMENT LAB

SCOOP
HOTLINE

MONDAY.
AMAZING. SEEMS LIKE I GOT SOME INTERESTING SHOTS AFTER ALL. WELL, OF COURSE, I ALWAYS KNEW I WOULD. THE MOLENSKI INVESTIGATIVE ANTENNA NEVER REALLY STOPS WORKING. THE PAPER'S SELLING LIKE CRAZY.
THE DAILY ROAR
SCOOP!
WRONG-FOOTED! BIGFOOT BROUGHT TO HEEL
By our reporter, Monty Molenski
THE DAILY ROAR
SCOOP!
HI SPIRITS! GHOSTS BUSTED
An EXCLUSIVE by ace reporter, Monty Molenski
WE'RE SICK TO DEATH!
GIVE OUR BONES BACK!
TUESDAY.
AT LAST, I'M OFFICIALLY 'ACE' REPORTER AT THE DAILY ROAR.
ABOUT TIME!

WEDNESDAY.
THE NATIONAL PAPERS ARE CALLING ME 'REPORTER OF THE CENTURY'! MY PHONE HASN'T STOPPED RINGING AND I'M GOING TO BE ON TELLY TONIGHT! (MUST GET MUM TO SET THE VIDEO.)
THE DAILY ROAR
SCOOP!
LOOK! NESSIE!
SEE SERPENT IN CITY POND
ONTY MOLENSKI EXCLUSIV

THE DAILY ROAR
SCOOP!
BY MOLENSKI
THE KING AND I –
ELVIS LIVES!
Suspicious minds proved correct
THE DAILY ROAR
BY MOL
THE KIN
ELVIS
Suspicious minds
THURSDAY.
THEY'RE GOING TO MAKE A FILM OF MY LIFE!

FRONT PAGE
ROAR
SCOOP!
HI SPIRITS!
GHOSTS BUSTED
An EXCLUSIVE by Monty Molenski.
MONTY MOLENSKI
THE DAILY
ROAR
SCOOP!
FOOTED!

CLUB

THE DAILY ROAR

SCOOP!

LOOK! NESSIE!

SEE SERPENT IN CITY POND

A MONTY MOLENSKI EXCLUSIVE.

FRIDAY.

AT THE END OF AN EXHAUSTING WEEK, THE EDITOR PERSONALLY WELCOMED ME INTO THE F.P. CLUB.

FINALLY MY TALENTS HAVE BEEN RECOGNISED! I THINK I SHOWED GREAT DIGNITY AS I ACCEPTED MY AWARD.

THE ED'S NOT A BAD CHAP, REALLY. MAYBE I JUDGED HIM TOO HARSHLY BEFORE — HE'S NOT SUCH A MONSTER AFTER ALL...

THE END?